Weaving W
The Poetry and Thougl

© Elle Mort

I dedicate this book to the people I love most. My muse, my family and circle of close friends. Also, those friends on social media who have interacted with me when I have shared my poetry and given me the self-confidence to continue writing.

To Joe & Erica, Paddy & Jennifer, Natalie, Georgina, Shella and Sara and Beryl, thank you from the bottom of my heart for your acceptance of me. May our tribe prosper and be always filled, with love.

To my circle of beautiful friends, Susan, Gillian, Steph, Sandra, Esmee and Frankie you are warriors and an inspiration to me. To Dave, thank you for the 'kick up the bum' I needed to get this book out there, and for all your hard work in making it so. To my muse, thank you for your perfections and your flaws, they live in my work as a reminder. Always.

I love you all, to the moon and back.

Foreword

I'm delighted to have been invited to write the forward to this book. Not only is Elle a personal friend, but she is also an inspiration. When I first read her poetry, I recognised a rare talent for she is a wordsmith and spellbinder. Elle Mort has a special gift for creating imagery, but her work and words are much more than that, she touches emotions and strokes the soul. Elles messages and insights into the human condition are not always gentle and are often ambiguous.
She weaves her Wyrd Path through ancestral voices most cannot hear. She taps dimensions most are not aware exist, she walks in the shadows of unseen worlds through her words.
I have been moved to tears and then chilled by her words as they leap out from the page.
If I have to sum up how I feel about her writing, I can only do this through the use of such words as otherworldly, soulful, emotional, ethereal and sometimes dark and chilling. She has a rare gift for looking into, and through the soul in all, it's colours and conditions.
I am her biggest fan, I am immensely proud to be her friend, I admire her inner

strength which manifests through her poetry, and I celebrate the fact that Weaving Wyrd has, at last, been made available to everyone.

The Poetry and Thoughts of Elle Mort aren't all they appear, they go much deeper into the human psyche and play with the reader as we walk that path of Wyrd with her characters

You may even recognise yourself in her poems and thoughts.

Thank you, Elle, for your friendship and a bond that goes deeper.

This is a wonderful collection of poems to treasure. Already I look forward to the second book.

Gill Smith.

Introduction

Ever since I can remember, poetry has been part of my life. The words and the flow come easy to me, like the rhythm of the music.

It brings me immense joy in happy times and soothes me, even in the darkest nights of the soul.

It is my constant companion; my words pour out on the page almost as quickly as they are created in my brain.

We all have a dark side, but there is a balance in us. Mine manifests in ink rather than deed.

If I can write poetry, you can do it too. You don't need a captive audience; you don't even need to have talent. The most important thing is that you write it for yourself; you don't need to share it with anyone if you don't want to. All you must do, is to be honest, use your love, use your pain in your writing.

Words are healing; they can be a tool to release negativity inside when you make them manifest on a page.

Do not fear to walk in the darkest of places, You will be a beacon of hope in the caverns and the shadows.

The City of Screaming Pyres

No poet ever found his muse
Within these city walls.
Too desolate and damaged
Too many clarion calls.

The winding streams of whimsy
Are red and choked with blood.
Pretences of humanity
Were banished in the flood.

Where beauty reigned so long ago
All is now flawed and scarred.
The Churches smashed, iconoclasts
Have left the temples marred.

~~~~~~~

We all carry ghosts around.
They are but the memories
Of our lost hopes and aspirations.
The things we wish we had done differently.
The things we would change
If we could.
They haunt us in the twilight before sleep
And in the misty morning
When all feels unnatural.
They cry out to us in dreams
Why?
We see them reflected back
In the eyes of other people.
They mock us from the achievements
Of our contemporaries.
If we give them power
They can permeate our souls,
And ooze misery from our pores,
Or we can lay them to rest
And not mourn for their passing.

~~~~~~~~

As you lay sleeping in the earth
I set a stone Angel to watch over you.
To stare forever with sightless eyes.
With a heart as empty as mine,
And cold as the snow.

You left me far to soon,
Before my love faded.
Before I could despise the passage of time
In the lines on your face.
Before I caused your tears.

I sit here watching your Angel.
Her features are composed.
When her beauty fades
And is pitted by the rain
I will come no longer.

All things have a season.
They are cruel and fleeting.
I cannot forgive you.
For dying before I hated you
And leaving me alone.

~~~~~~~

She pulled down the dark velvet of the night.
Embroidered it and with truth and light.
Stitched it with tears and kisses
And good intent.
She made a blanket, filled with love.
It surrounded all who surrendered to her care.
A thousand flowers grew when she laid it on the ground,
Each one was named hope.
And when they opened, an awakening was found
Even on the stoniest ground.
The stars from the universe were stuck to her hair
From when she reached across the veil.
The song of the spheres
Forever in her heart on and on her lips.

~~~~~~~

We clashed, under the illusion of gaslight
When you couldn't cope with my life.
You tried your own take on Deus ex Machina
But the only person who would have been
happy
With the ending, would have been you.

You used psychology as a weapon,
Wielding a passive aggressive shield.
You thought yourself above discovery.
Only you failed to convince me
That I was the victim of my own psyche.

The only forces at work
Were your egotistical machinations.
Resulting in a fail of epic proportions.
I survived you intact!

And as our paths diverge, I am stronger.
Not vulnerable as you hoped.
Being haunted by the living
Is more draining than anything the dead have
to offer.

~~~~~~~~

Trees stand sentinel
In shadow
On the brow of the hill.
Like dark soldiers
Awaiting command.
Stretching out branches
Instead of hands.
While tendrils of fog
Creep silently over
The frozen ground.
Awaiting a lone traveller
To caress with cold fingers
While the moon watches sadly.
A dumb witness through time
With the power to light
But not to warm.
The crunch of the frosty soil
Is a warning.
It cries 'Go back'
In a language so ancient
That we cannot understand.

~~~~~~~

After the flood has receded
The water's damage can be seen.
While you are submerged
The rust doesn't show.
Only when the sun shines on it
Once more
The cracks in the foundation
That underpin your sanity
Are gaping like an open wound.
Infection is likely and expected daily.
Cross contamination
From other damaged vessels.
What is your agenda?
It was never a question I asked
When I followed you.
Under the influence of Morpheus.
Disguised as spirituality.
A fog that made it easy to step in a mire.
Unseeing.
Bogged down suddenly
With no lifeline.
No desire to escape.
Until your shadow was exposed
Of everything you took from me.
The hardest to come to terms with
Is that you took my trust.
Fragility was but a plaything for you.
Like a cat tormenting its prey.
You damage wings bit by bit

So your quarry cannot fly.

~~~~~~~

The watcher at the gates
of the Otherworld awaits.
Biding his time by playing on the threads
Made from the strands of our Wyrd.
Making music which pulls our heartstrings
And heals us in spirit as we cry.
Gentle as the rain.
Our souls drawn to the beating drum of
The changing of the seasons.
Green and gold
Have passed us by now.
The silvers and whites have come
In our hair and on the land.
The wind whispers his name
Can you hear it?
Lost to you in the mists of time
It caresses you when you sleep.
An enigma to be found
In dream time.
Forgotten when you wake.
You will remember when
The watcher greets you
At the gates.

~~~~~~~

Your light never flickered or went out,
It just moved from the world into our hearts
To shine as brightly as you shone in life.
The beauty of your laughter
Will never fade from our ears.
Years may pass,
But when we hear your name
A smile will be on our lips.
Sleep well my darling one,
You brought us so much joy.
The music of the universe will be yours
For eternity,
There for you to dance to through time.

~~~~~~~

I love the idea of you
When the moon is full
And in my dreams
I'm yearning for your face
To be held within my hands.
I worship every thought of you.
Your smile illuminates the page of every book I
read.
Soft as candle light stirring my soul.
When dawn comes there is reality
As harsh as the morning sun on sleepy eyes.
I cannot be with you
I will not give up this life less extraordinary.
No portent is dire enough
To warn me of your imminent loss.

I will not pick a rose for you.
Even though they grow plentiful in my garden,
And your once full chocolate box is empty now
But slowly filling with your tears.
All the caresses you say are vital
I will withhold.
You live for me in my desires and
Not in my routines.
You are the hope in my Pandora's Box.
But I fear to set you free in case your wings
should open,
And your beauty metamorphosize for another.
I will keep you imprisoned

With the occasional desultory kindness
So you cannot become whole for another.

~~~~~~~

The hope in Pandora's box
Has been dormant too long
Will fluttering white wings
Emerge wholesome?
Or will they be tarnished
With rust and dust?
Will the wings still work?
Can they be lubricated
With WD40 or tears?
As a testament to wasted years
When I waited in the shadows
Afraid to walk in light
Can I learn to use the wings?
Dare I?

~~~~~~~~

You want to play games?
Let's play 'Who's soul is more toxic?'
You ask me what that is.
Well you should know
It's your invention.
Necessity didn't feature
Just ego.

If I was breastfed guilt
You must have imbibed poison.
It oozes from your pores.
Hangs on your every sibilant syllable,
And drops when you are sure
The wound is open
Drip by drip.

~~~~~~~

Fear

Foreshadowed and sometimes foreboding.
Always forbidding and never forgotten.
Tentacles of frost with freezing fingers
Feel for my fatal flaws,
Finding them, they fashion a fearsome grip.
Finally fleeing when reason flies back.
Scuttling furtively, back to their lair.
Fermenting feverishly until they flit back.
My mind is never free of their fiendish forms.
Plethora's of Priests have pursued me.
Pressing me with prose from Psalms.
Pretending they aren't empty platitudes.
Presenting me with unwanted pity
While I played at psychosis
And found it pleasing.

~~~~~~~~

The fractured pieces
From all the fragile people you destroy
Hang from your aura like a parody of medals.
Your room is painted with the blood of slit
wrists
From your razor blade psyche.

Come closer now, closer.
I have been the fly to your spider.
Swallow me now
I am so full of antidepressants
I will poison you.

Tables are turned.
You left me without empathy.
Sucked me dry of it.
Now it is your turn to reciprocate.
You made me die inside.

~~~~~~~

Hedge your bets

It's that moment of disconnection
When everything is so clear
You can taste the arcane
But it dissolves too quickly
To retain memory

It's what you see
Periphery
The seconds of pure
Clarity
A lifetime of
Insanity

Faces in branches are not pareidolic
Consciousness is breached
The mists are ephemeral
Like an aura in the eye
Illusionary fantasy

Returning to
Reality
You face your own
Mortality
And live with your
Duality

~~~~~~~~

You are as dark as an alter-ego.
Your eyes are windowless
Because your soul fled long ago
From all who tried to love you

Your smile is saccharine
The sweetness replaced by E numbers
Tasty for seconds but false
The after-taste too acerbic

Your make-up masks the lines of discontent
upon your brow
The bitterness mars your once plump lips
Kissable no longer
At least not by me

Instead of mellowing like a fine wine
In your impatience, you used immature berries
And your brew became toxic
Lethal to all who sip from your poison chalice

Your mansion is devoid of love
No fledglings share your nest
Teaching them to fly
Would have cost you effort

There are cracks in your foundation
The ugliness you seek to camouflage
Is seeping through

Plain for all to see now

You demanded gratitude for your attention
Whilst isolating me from all I held dear
The pedestal you created for others to worship
you
Has fractured from the weight of your ego

~~~~~~~~

You are all alone now
My, what have you done?
Caught up in your own thread
Of all the lies you've spun

You saw no consequences
They came, nevertheless
You just took me for granted
As someone to suppress

How do you feel now darling?
Now the worm and table turned?
Are you blowing on your fingers?
After they got burned?

From the tatters of your empire
Where all is lost and wrecked
Do you ever realise
It came from your neglect?

~~~~~~~~

I tended the garden of your soul.
Planted some exquisite flowers.
Landscaped you exotic bowers.
Grew lilies in your fountain bowl.

The fragile petals were preserved.
I nurtured soil and planted seeds.
Coppiced and pulled up the weeds.
It was more than you deserved.

Like bindweed with intrusive shoots.
With my gardening you tampered.
Cold tendrils spread and hampered.
They choked the life out of the roots.

Your soul garden is overgrown.
It yields no fruit nor bud or bean.
There's not a blossom to be seen.
Not since my role was overthrown.

~~~~~~~

I am the whisper in your ear
That magnifies your every fear

The adder on the wooded path
The deathly virus aftermath

I am the ice patch in the snow
The current in the waters flow

The carpet frayed upon the stair
The fall that takes you unaware

I am the footfall in the dark
The twilight lurker in the park

The heavy breathing on your phone
The noises when you're home alone

~~~~~~~

I am lost without you.
You are the other half of my whole.
We have been brought together
On the wings of the Goddess.
You are the thought to my memory.
The wood to my rune.
My wand becomes a staff
When I hold you in my arms.

Do you feel it too, little one?
Have you heard the higher calling?
The Gods speak to me.
They tell me we are destined
To lay together
Beneath the moon
In the here and now.
I will take you with no thought
For the father of your children.

I am the Taliesin of my age.
Only I hold the knowledge
Your soul needs to move onwards.
We can explore it together
From our hotel room.
Are you mine yet?
Only mine?
Would you cast aside your husband?
To be my Twin Flame?

I hear you whisper "Yes"
And I am sated
You utterly surrendered
Gave me all, so I tell you
The Goddess speaks to me now
Tells me I should respect you
Set you free to walk your path
To return to the world bereft
Without me.

So many soul mates await me.
In the flame of the path I pretend to.
My self-esteem is measured
In the tears of my victims.
The destruction of the families.
The stripping of your spirituality.
But it feeds my ego
That is all that matters.
I knock you down.
There are dozens to take your place.

~~~~~~~

You are becoming!
Metamorphosis is just
A heartbeat away.
Never ever let
A moment of regret
Pass through fleetingly.
What you will be
Is whole.
So leave the past willingly.
Take from it, only the lessons
You learned with tears,
And the love
Gathered through the years.
Put it all to good use.
Let the pain go.
It will not serve you here.
Nor will anger and fear.

~~~~~~~~

I am in the wild place
A garden of twisted vines
A forest of synapses
Forever intertwined

Hanged on the ash tree
With memory and thought
While comfort and charity
All come to nought

I've made sacrifices
Of both love and kindness
Given up for darker things
Like jealousy and blindness

Knowledge burns inside of me
Seared inside my soul
For that purpose, I traded
That which I can't control

~~~~~~~

Just because the path is lit with moonbeams
The destination will be no less dark

~~~~~~~

You are bedecked with jasmine flowers
White and waxy as your skin.
Perfectly preserved beauty
With eyes forever closed.
Cold to the touch.
The flush of your cheeks a memory.
Lips pale beneath a rosy tint.
I touch them one last time.
You will be gone from me
After one last vigil.
I hold your hand
Through the chimes of midnight
Till the dawn breaks,
And you will lie in the ground
Alone, for there I cannot follow.
I will lay the rose on the wood
With a handful of graveyard soil
And hide my tears behind a veil.

~~~~~~~

Magic seeps onward t'ward Llyn Tegid shore.
Shrouded in legend, in mystery and lore.
Ceridwen is weeping, her cauldron is cracked.
She cries for Afagddu for beauty he lacked.
Her rage knows no boundary, she plucks
Morda's eye.
Turns into a hawk and she takes to the sky.
Chasing down Gwion, who turns to a grain.
Swallows him whole when a hen she became.
The grain it took root in Ceridwen's own womb.
And the babe born in nine moons she cast to
his doom.
Caught was the child in the nets at a weir.
And he grew to be wise, a great bard and a
seer.

~~~~~~~~

Come weave your magic in bright strands
Upon the concrete of this land.
Let car parks crack with brown tree roots
And pavements hide in new green shoots.

Let office blocks be ivy clad.
Motorways with vines grow mad.
Ancient paths not modern roads.
Grass will cover new abodes.

The fox and badger running free
Never more will hunted be.
Wild flower multiply in fields
Instead of the GM crop yield.

Ancient waters cold and clean
Not fluoride ridden or obscene.
This can happen with one plan.
Eliminate the greed of man.

Walk with light within your heart
Against injustice, do your part.
When others fall, hold out your hand
Live lightly on the good green land.

~~~~~~~

A thousand voices reach me.
Each one with love on their lips.
"You are more than the sum of us" they cry
And enfold me in their arms of mist.

~~~~~~~~

Pan will call you home
On lilting pipes.
You will hear, the sounds of nostalgia.
Music woven in leaves
Like a cloak of forest green.
The wild woods are waiting.
Come in.
There is magic here.
It is cool and carefree.
You can dance like a child again.
No woes or worries.
The sun is gentle.
The trees will embrace you
Like a long-lost lover.
I will be waiting
In the shadows.
You will listen to the wind
Whisper your name.
We can lie together
Under the canopy of stars.
When twilight melts to night
The fireflies will give us light
Up until the dawn.

~~~~~~~

When we met
You had the aura of cigarette smoke
And desperation.
Drinking bitter black coffee
In a bookshop.
Reading the classics.
Promoting a lifestyle
You never had.
Living on the edge of the fringe.
Never a part of it.
Nobody was fooled.

~~~~~~~~

Hiraeth

I'm the companionable silence
by the hearth you've never seen.
I am the whisper on the wind
That calls from where you've never been.

The siren song, across the seas
that only you can hear.
The secret place within your heart
Where there is no fear.

I'm the love of a thousand ancestors
Who lived and died before.
The face you see within the flames
As the bone fires roar.

I am the hand that takes your own
When all around you fails.
The memory of your past life
In long lost fairy tales.

I am the genius loci
From the land you've never known.
I am the calling of your blood
Come to lead you home.

I'm every small compulsion
That makes your spirit yearn.

I am the light within your soul
That guides you to return.

~~~~~~~

Outcast and alone.
Nowhere to call home.
The Otherworld calls
From the darkened portals.
So I go to the fires
And the funeral pyres.
I talk to the dead
With no sense of dread.
The shades are my friends
When the madness descends.

~~~~~~~

I have spent my life
Weaving the threads of wyrd
I have spun them
Into tapestry
Colours as bright as jewels
Interwoven with darkness
Have started to unravel
As time goes on
Some scenes have nearly faded now
But others remain
I can hear music as I look on them
In crystal clarity
Sorrowful scenes intercept it
In places
Drawn and stitched
In painful monochrome
They have often been washed
With my tears
Flowers in the picture
Are facsimiles of those
Presented with love
The scent still interwoven
Into the fabric
The tapestry is unique
Aspects might be the same
As those sewn by others
But never the whole scene
It is my segment alone
Although it is joined

to the panels of those
My threads have entwined with others
Who have walked beside me
Briefly or over thousands of leagues
Some are snagged or frayed
But others hold fast
If they become unwholesome
They can be cut away

~~~~~~~

Weave with the Wyrd you are given
Frame your life into tapestry

~~~~~~~

I've spent my day gathering
rue and yarrow
from the grasslands
Bitter as graveyard soil
cold as the corpse of regret
Yet the yarrow will heal the pain
the rue has wrought
Eventually....

~~~~~~~

Many cut themselves just to feel
I cut my soul
And the words contained within
bleed onto the page
Leaving a tiny part of me in every poem
DNA in ink
Fragile but not brittle
Full of my psyche
Bare, for all to see

~~~~~~~~

The walls in shadow
Whisper to me
In gloom's half light.
Voices from beyond the veil
Trapped in the bricks
Forever in a loop of sadness.
I feel the anger
When I touch the wall.
The sadness remains.
Reaching out
Full of tears
A vortex of power
Silent for years
With the promise
Of violence.
Never far from the surface
An undertow hidden
In a millpond.
But surfacing in dreams
And visions
To ensnare you
In an icy grip
Of chaos.
The smell of funeral flowers
Comes and goes
The wind sings dirges
Full of sinister promise
But beautiful
Reminding me

You are there

~~~~~~~

I'm drawn to the places
Where I can hide
Be less than nothing
Secure and insulated
From worldly hatred
The shadow lands
Of my mind
There are dark places
And I explore
They attract and repel
In equal measures
The crawling things
Can be beautiful too
I cloak myself in them
But don't let them within
I can remain pure here
With no willpower
My armour was forged
From the falsehood of others
It has served me well
I have taken no mortal wound
As my ego was chipped away
Over half a lifetime
I've no hate left
For those who damaged me
And left me less than whole

~~~~~~~

If I could take a crystal
And store our memories inside
I would hold it up to the sun
Every day, to see your picture.
I would wear it always,
Next to my heart
To feel your essence
Close by.
It would be made from quartz
Smoky like your eyes.
After we made love
I would gaze at it
And remember our first time
When you cried tears of joy
On our release
And hear the music, playing low
On the old stereo.
I would trade my soul
To protect the clarity
Of my knowledge of you

~~~~~~~

My soul is walking
in the hidden places.
The hollow ways
And the Herepaths,
The roads of the dead
On the final journey
To fall to dust
Within their tomb
In charnel houses.
I have seen
The piles of bone
Amongst the stone
Crossroad graves.
Souls unsaved.
The Wild Hunt calls.

~~~~~~~

The Ballad of Alice Bellringer

The crystal catches the last of the evening light
And gently kisses you on the face with a
rainbow
Softly fading to nothing as the clouds come
Leaving a memory of the fleeting beauty of the
sun
The autumn leaf that falls from the tree
Sacrificed itself to the crunch under your shoe
I heard it did so willingly
Even the spider weaves her web
In the coldest of places, so that frost diamonds
Gleam for you in the morning
Before they melt away to nourish the plants
In the frozen soil of your wilderness
Flowers bloom with jewelled colour
Among the canopy of shelter, like faerie lights
The heady perfume of jasmine will bathe you
As you walk upon the land
The twilight cloaks you gently in her velvet
As the moon rises, just to light you on your
way.

~~~~~~~~

When you are in the cemetery
And passing by my grave
Stop a while and talk to me
Your company I crave

I long to hear you speak my name
My family are all gone
Nobody left, to tend my grave
My memory can't live on

Except for a line, upon a branch
Of someone's family tree
Those I have known have all moved on
So none remember me

Thank you for your company
For here I must remain
To hear my name upon your lips
Has made me live again

~~~~~~~

Just for today, leave me the flowers
Their petals fade with time on the altar of your
love
They will stay and become a dusty impression
Into nothing
Sorrow is overrated
Promises also
Made to be broken
Premeditated sacrifice is no sacrifice at all
Weighing up what you can afford to lose
Lacks the spontaneity of honesty
The roses are the ones who sacrificed
They will never die back to be reborn now
It is them I grieve for
They will never live again
The cycle is broken
Dead, by your hand
So leave them and walk away
I will be their tombstone

~~~~~~~

I am the chime child
The liminal one
Who's foretelling came
With the ring of bells
Always in between the worlds
A foot in each
Cauled of aura
Bereft of kin
Fey and wild
Walls contain only memory
They cannot contain me
One touch of you
And I can see your soul
The blackness you hide
Is my playground
Your sins are manna
I feed from them gladly
Your prayers cannot save you
From one such as me
Light your candles
And smudge your sage
It is of no benefit
You cannot hurt me
The mists protect me
Shrouded in secrets I am

~~~~~~~

Make me a cake full of secrets
Mix it with a mystery
Layer it with history
Bake it until it is done
Then cool it and ice
With the sugar and spice
Of your memories

~~~~~~~

You invite me to your fancy dress party?
I'll come wearing my scars
Shamelessly
I can always say they are as fake
(as your interest in them would be)
If you could see further than your own nose

Seriously
You were born to dress up
Your true personality is usually disguised
From the crowd
Under the right conditions
When it gets too heated for comfort
The make-up slides
Gradually

And that which lies beneath
Shows through

~~~~~~~

The Wildhunt of Outcast Souls

WE ARE COMING, they scream
You thought us less than human
Undeserving of an afterlife without torment
We are the pauper
The stolen corpse
Those left under highways
And crossroads
Those of us who were nameless
Before your God
Are blameless
Our fate decided by Kirk and Crown
Laid down below unhallowed sod
If we are doomed to wander
Without comfort
Don't think to sleep the sleep
Of the innocent
We had no marker to point our way
To Heaven or to Hell
But in your dreams, we dwell
We walk together now
The iron in our hearts
Transmuted to will
As we ride the veil that cloaks us

~~~~~~~

You missed the bus
Ran too late to catch it
Because your ship didn't come in
You realised too late
That the comfortable upholstery
Was a better choice
Than shiny, cold leather
Unyielding beneath you
The price tag was just too much
You could only look, not touch
You missed the bus

~~~~~~~

Sarah of the Crossroads

The comfort of Gods arms denied you
The walls of the Church never yours
In life or in death
A broken promise
Took away your will to live
Those who should have aided you
In your pain
Turned you away
They cast you aside because you loved
Unwisely
Cast you into unhallowed ground
At crossroads
Millions have passed you by
Unaware
But we know you lay there
Flowers we will bring
John and I
We will speak your name
With love
Not as one on the edge of society
But with love, as distant family
Your soul holds no stain
Sleep gently in the womb of the ground
May the rain wash away your pain
You are not forgotten
The snowdrops that grow on your grave
Are your tribute

~~~~~~~

There is no greater crime than to rewrite
history
To scrub the pages with bleach
And start again with a clean slate
Burn the books
pretend it didn't happen

Sanitise them
Change the ending
Rather than move on and do better
In the future
At least that would be honest

Learn from our mistakes
Rather than reinvent the past
Revisionism is worse than the sin
We try to cover up

It's like painting over a still life
With an impressionist piece
And declaring the original a forgery
We are only fooling ourselves really

~~~~~~~~

Can't you see I'm broken?
I try and tell you without words
Every day
In lots of ways
Don't you recognise the look
In my eyes?
Is it beyond your scope of vision?
To see my pain?
When I say "I'm okay"
Again, and again
To always be 'the strong one'
Is tiring sometimes
The one relied upon
To mend
My friends
The hand holding yours
Is full of pain some days
The mouth that gives advice
Must sacrifice
The chance to speak out

~~~~~~~

The inky blackness embraced you
Like the flame embraces the moth
The stars were the only diamonds
You needed to adorn you
You were born knowing
Your true nature
And how to conceal it
Behind enigmatic eyes
While others strived
To find their inner balance
Yours came as naturally
As the sunrise in the morn
None would have guessed your depths
Unless they were drowning in your wake
Midnight is your name, twilight is your time
The shadows are your playground

~~~~~~~

Moon Child

How can one born to darkness shine so?
The moon knows my madness
And bathes me in memories
Bittersweet, a blessing and a curse
I rifle through to find a point of reference
It is there, fleeting then denied
I search when she is full
To find the form of my Goddess
And never manage to hold the image
For more than a moment
Just long enough to tantalise
And wish for the old closeness to return
Even though the glimpse of heaven
Is clothed in velvet and stars
It lacks the warmth of a cloak
And the lustre it once held for me
Yet still I gaze
In hope

~~~~~~~

We are blank sheets of paper
When we come into the world
As soon as we take our first breath
We have additions to our marginalia
What weight were we?
What time were we born?
This is added to over the years
We should be able to cherish every word
Curly calligraphy
Merged with hearts
Treated with love and kindness
Never scribbled on in haste
Or screwed up and cast aside
Or put in a notepad with other paper
Only chosen occasionally
And written on in a whim
With slapdash hands
Or torn and ripped
In careless or cruel treatment
But handled with care
Even when the paper is sepia with age

~~~~~~~~

Do we ever reflect upon the honour
Of walking in the dust of ancient civilisations?
In the shadows of our ancestors
Our steps in the footprint of theirs
Our hands touching the same stones?
Your tree of life has branches on
With our ancestors as leaves
That have floated to the ground
And become renewed
The roots go deep and grow strong
When we nurture them
They are our roots too
As what went before is intertwined
With now
Plant your own tree
And strengthen it with love
Remember the names of those gone before
And write the names of those still to come
In the stars
Do not mourn the fallen leaves for long
For when they fall, they feed the roots
And become immortal
They are etched in your memory
Instead, share their story
All falls eventually, save love

~~~~~~~

You have grown cold
As I have grown old
Like I am less now
Than once I was
Your indifference measured
By inches on my waist
And lines on my face
If you unwrapped me
As a gift
You would ask
For the receipt
Return me as faulty
But now I'm out of guarantee
I'm worthless to you
You can't even trade me in
For a newer model
The truth be known
I deteriorated under
The lack of maintenance
For something to stand
The test of time
Regular care
And careful handling
Are needed
You provided neither

~~~~~~~~

Ice Maiden

When the first flakes of snow
Came drifting slowly down
They fell just like confetti
Upon your bridal crown

You were reposed and elegant
Even in your death
Shrouded by the freezing air
Of winters ragged breath

I kept vigil over you
All throughout that night
Watchful, still and silent
Bathed in pale moonlight

~~~~~~~

Your face was bathed in moonbeams
Your skin as white as milk
Your eyes were bright as emeralds
Your hair as soft as silk

I lay you down in pasture
Where mountain meets the sea
Adorned your cloak in meadow flowers
Before I set you free

~~~~~~~

Drumming for war
Oiling the cogs
Of the unstoppable machine
It marches forward
Regardless of pity
Visiting the nameless
And the faceless
With more stealth
Than the Reaper
Trading souls
For commodities
Innocence or guilt
Immaterial
They die regardless
Regarded as collateral
Relegated to cattle
To be culled at will
Is the pain of a family
Any less
If a death is under the banner
Of friendly fire?
Does that make it right?
Is a dictator with oil
Worse than one without?
Vainglorious leaders
Want a legacy
Rather than working
For the common good
They carve their name

In bleached bones in the desert
It will become synonymous
With bloodshed
But remembered nonetheless
They can clean the gore away
Hoover up the resources left behind
But the blood remains on their hands
Stained like their souls
Only peace begets peace

~~~~~~~

The Age of Aquarius

The cacophony from the portals
Screams from the other side
Muted now to incoherent whispers
By the veil
Muffled messages are no longer clear
Thousands of voices
Drown out the words of one
The lines of communication
Are down, but not out
The world still turns
But the scrying stone is dark
The crystal is cloudy
Atrocity abounds
Balance is shaky
Even on common ground
Agendas are hidden
With flimsy disguise
Slipping further away
With every heartbeat
The scales weighted
In favour of the warmongers
Who cheat by using
The wealth of the few
Which is heavier
Than the tears of the many
They worship the 'Profit'
At the Temple of Futures

The bear and the bull
No longer sacrificial
Are golden idols
Vainglorious leaders
Wage war in our name
Where the only flags they fly
By our standards are false
Politicians without attrition
Say a tearless farewell to
Democracy rather than arms

~~~~~~~

Ode to 'Shamers' Everywhere

And what makes you the expert on others?
The way they choose to live their lives
To style their hair
Their body shape and sexuality
Are you perfect?
I'm sure the answer to that
Is a resounding 'No'
Casting stones is dangerous
When your own life is made of the same glass
One might rebound
And put cracks in your confidence
Didn't your mother tell you
"If you can't say something nice, don't say
anything at all"?
It was probably the best advice she ever gave
you
I'm sure the people you deride
Are more beautiful than you inside
Is there something so lacking in your soul
That makes you cruel and hard?
Judging people on the content of their wardrobe
And dress size
Rather than the size of their heart
You fall short, not them
You are the imperfect one
As you lack humanity
The milk of kindness you lactate

Is sour and bitter
Take a good look at yourself
Your glasses are tinted with bile
Not roses

~~~~~~~

It's that black hole in your centre
That opens up
To all the pain and negativity
The world has to offer
And sucks it in.
The controls are broken,
You cannot close it
Nor know why the dam is open.
It wasn't a choice
But a malfunction
Without human error.
Others tell you
To turn off the switch
And it will stop,
But there is no switch,
Just autopilot
And you are pulled along
In the slipstream,
Unable to get free
From its momentum.
Until one day
The hole starts to close
And the pain begins
To recede,
Slowly.
Never all at once
But even when it shuts
You are aware the
Repair might not be permanent,

That cracks could start to appear
Any time
And the panic might come back.
No finger is needed
To trigger it
It just IS!
And regardless of intent
Nobody is immune from it.
It will pass
And the days will again
Be full of laughter.
But take my hand
When I feel like
The world must surely end.
Just
Be my friend.

~~~~~~~

Are you going to host a pity party?
Send out the invites
You will be the only guest
Crack open the bottle
What's your poison?
Arsenic, I hope
Your life, your rules
You made me jump
Through hoops made
From Mindfulness
When your sensitivity
Is the rhino in the room
In more ways than one

~~~~~~~

When all around you is falling to pieces
And 'This too shall pass'
When the world seems devoid of love
And divide and conquer rules
Remember 'This too shall pass'
When the darkness in knocking at your door
And the shadows seem to take on life
Just light your inner candle
Because 'This too shall pass'
When the long night of the soul is here
Tormenting you in dire times
Look inside your very soul
Find the love you thought was lost
For 'This too shall pass'

~~~~~~

All things will rust
If they aren't loved
They become derelict
With lack of care
Tread lightly
On the broken stair
Or your fall may come
Too soon

Wipe the dust
From your eyes
Kiss the stars
Appreciate the light
From the sun
And beams from the moon
As it may fade
Too soon

Hold that you love
Close to you
Maintain it
With regularity
And thoughtful deeds
And empathy
Then it may not decay
Too soon

~~~~~~~

In that split second
Which lasts,
Somewhere between
The blink of an eye
And infinity.
Life can change
In one random act of chaos.
Everything you know
(or think you understand)
Can vanish into dust
And what you thought
Was unbreakable
Is insubstantial,
Like thistledown
In a storm,
Leaving despair
In its wake.

~~~~~~~

You spent my life
Telling me I was not good enough.
You hit me again and again
Until you thought I was broken.
You see
The thing about the cracks
You made in me
Is that they allow my inner light
To shine through.
I can live in your darkness
Understand the torture of souls
And let them bleed on a virgin page.
Your very nature made me
The opposite of you.
Your nemesis!
Because your control
Spiralled away
And diminished you
In my eyes.

~~~~~~~

Trick or treat?
You decide
Are you sure now?
Positive?
Can I decide the treat?
Describe it to you?
It will be red and viscous
copious in amount
but sadly limited
to eight pints per person.
Would you care
to sample the candy?
I made it myself!
It is laden with good things.
They say a spoonful of sugar
helps the medicine go down
(the barbiturates are bitter
without it).

~~~~~~~

I Died Today

But only inside
when the hand
that should have reached out
and taken mine
did not

As we lay on the bed
there is a whole ocean between us
If I try to cross that distance
I will drown
or you will capsize me
with just a word

We each occupy a piece of land
on the edge
we staked claim to it
long ago
the territory is marked
non-negotiable, but tacit
no need of contracts
verbal or written

There are too many weapons
in your arsenal
they may be blunt
but capable nonetheless
of wounding

My desire for crossing
into uncharted space
is diminishing with time
each attempt
making me more weary
I have given up
believing that one day
you would meet me
in the middle
for more than a day trip
With your own itinerary
and the agenda
unclear
at least to me

~~~~~~~

Bonefire of the Insanities

Transient liminality
One foot in sanity
The other in the abyss

Fascinated and repelled
In equal measure
I am the grey
The shade between
Light and darkness

My screams are silent
Yet strangely soothing

"Cross to the light" you cry
"I cannot" I reply
I have been burned before

I still bear the scars
With dignity
I am of the night

~~~~~~~

I found the children of my imagination
Twins born of parthenogenesis
I named them Hope and Despair
I abandoned Hope a long time ago
In eternal spring
In favour of her brother
And the loss reigns heavy
On my leaded pain

~~~~~~~

All things shall pass
Some into legend
Others into obscurity
Memory lane is full
Of potholes and pitfalls
Revisit at your own risk
A chasm may appear
To suck you back in

~~~~~~~

Seeking approval, attention and need
You don't swim in the pond, on the bottom you feed
Courting a lifestyle that you enjoy
Self-harming and darkness is only a ploy

You befriend all the empaths that you can find
Target the vulnerable, leech from the kind
You show all the symptoms of total despair
If someone dug deeper, they'd see it's not there

Your ego is massive, your mindfulness low
The world is to blame for your own status quo
The innocent, targets for verbal assault
The fact you aren't happy is never your fault

You're so calculating, in all that you do
Not caring at all, what you put others through
You're transparent to me, though the words are unspoken
Nobody can fix you, because you aren't broken

~~~~~~~~

We live in the place
Where the dark and the light divide
We strive to live in the sun
And not the night
But the truth is, the twilight is where we are
And we cross the boundary's
With our thoughts (if not our deeds)

The darkness can be a good place
To face our demons
And come to an accord with them
If we stop exploring our true nature
We no longer grow
And if it means pain
We should embrace it
As without the balance
We lose sight of our soul

We make our own mask
Manufactured by the sum of our flaws
But no matter how well constructed
It will slip with time
Revealing our true nature
To ourselves
The mirror is only as dark
As our reflection

~~~~~~~

Profundis

We pulled down the temples stone by stone
de-constructed the mysteries
in our ignorance
when it was our time to shine
we chose the shade
frightened of burning too brightly
and the balefires that lit our souls
were quenched by tears of fear
that ran like waterfalls
within
things of the night
that were beautiful
became spectres of terror
we ran from them
and clothed ourselves in sackcloth
to scourge our sins
instead of embracing them
and our souls withered
the growth we should have attained
was stunted
by our own hands
we listened to the words of the priests
who taught us
to feel shame
we stopped the tribal dance
to the beat of the drums
in time with our hearts

in tune with the seasons
we knelt in silence instead
and the joy diminished
our ancestors weep for us
for all we have lost

~~~~~~~

I can walk the misty mountain pass
With impunity
I am not lost, I am found
In the light of the moon
I am where I need to be

Danger is subjective,
Adrenalin spurs me on
To darker things.
In the shadows I lurk
My own confusion lifted
By icy winds

The clarity of a psychopomp call
Leads me home.
Refreshed for a period
Until the elements call again
To leave my dusty room
And venture into twilight

If we met in misty mountains
I would mesmerise you
Pull you in and push you over
The very edge
Of desire

It may be mystic
Or monstrous maybe
Would you be maimed?

Or maybe enthralled?

Would we meet
On a chasms edge?
Would we struggle
On a ledge?

Do you have enough
Faith and trust?
A Damoclean decision Dear
But one you must make alone
I will not coerce you
Or will the unwilling
To the isolated place

With the shreds of my sanity
All but gone
What if you knew
A lone hair's breadth
Was all between
Your life and death?

~~~~~~~

Virtual Stockholm Syndrome

You chipped away
at the marble of my mind,
trying to sculpt me to your taste.
The chisel hurt less
than the weapon of your words.
I confused love with pain
until it grew unhealthy roots,
and choked and poisoned
healthy shoots.
For a time, I was a victim,
captive in a fantasy
that was never mine.
Folie à deux
is not in my remit.
I am better than that,
stronger.

~~~~~~~

96

Muse

My heart knew your voice
the very first time I heard it.
It was familiar as breathing.
It felt
like coming home.
The years flew away
and left me whole,

You are beautiful,
I love your perfection
and your flaws

Our souls connected
by invisible strings
which you now try to sever
at a mortal cost to me.

My love is unconditional.

I will accept the pain,
as it is better than nothing.

~~~~~~~

Stitch by stitch
the primal wound is healing
to be replaced by love.
Although I never knew
it was our separation
that caused the void,
it has always existed in me.

It was a well of tears,
an empty silence which should
always have been filled
with voices and laughter,
it has gone,
and the light has flooded in
golden like sunshine.

My heart whole for the first time,
because I have you
the reason for my being
You are
my first thought on waking,
my last thought before sleeping.
In my heart
and with me all the time
My soulmate.

~~~~~~~

The crystal waters
are muddied.
Clarity impaired
boundaries blurred,
nothing is clearly defined.

Things have come full circle,
back to self-doubt and rejection.
The only thing that changed
is that I let myself hope.
I should have known better

Perhaps it is something in me after all?
That makes people turn away

~~~~~~~

I'm going home
to a time of dragons,
a world of imagination
between pages
that are
creased with time.
My friends await me,
it has been a while
since our last visit.
Yet they are patient,
they don't berate me
for neglecting them
on a dusty shelf.
I'll be transported
into history's mists,
to better places
where magic exists,
I am safe there,
in my book.

~~~~~~~~

The grass,
which always looked greener to me,
called me to come.
So I left my comfortable pasture
and headed over a stony road,
navigating by the stars
only to find
it was decomposing
and rife with disease.
I toiled for years,
irrigated it with my tears,
but nothing grew
or thrived.
My soul withered,
along with the crops I planted,
while the land I'd abandoned
flourished.

~~~~~~~

I'm certain that the dead don't dance
beneath the moonlit skies,
I don't believe in fairy tales
because they're made up lies.

I don't believe in swords and cups
or once and future kings.
I put away all thoughts of Fae
and other childish things.

Now I work from an office desk,
with no chance to run wild,
and dream of dragons, elves and things,
like when I was a child.

~~~~~~~

The Night the Trees Danced

Llyn Tegid lit with sparkling lights
In water, tree and air.
One hundred voices joined in chant
In ceremony there

The Groves were faery grottos then
The trees they danced around,
When dawn light came and we could see
Their roots had left the ground

The Dryads heard our music sweet
And listened to our song
The Naiad's voices joined with ours
Harmony true and strong

In Otherworldly symphony
With those of Elder Race
Stood heart to heart and hand in hand
With the Spirit of the Place

~~~~~~~

I searched for her in the music
From the campfires near the trees
When I listened to the forest
Thought I heard her in the breeze

From standing stones, from hill and fen
She'll come again

She was reflected in the water
As I sat beside the well
Her face was shining in the ripples
Where she went I could not tell

From standing stones, from hill and fen
She'll come again

I saw her shadow by the window
As I cried out to the moon
And she whispered in the darkness
"You will find me very soon"

From standing stones, from hill and fen
She'll come again
From standing stone, from hill and fen
She'll come again

From standing stone, from hill and fen
She'll come again

~~~~~~~

I am made of cobwebs
with a little pixie dust
thrown in for good measure.
My wings are tattered gossamer
but that matters not,
as I cannot fly.

I'm in black lace, so dusty
that it looks grey with age.
It is my chrysalis,
I emerged as a moth
to darkness,
when I'd daydreamed
of becoming a butterfly.

Spending time in the sunlight
attracts me,
but there is a danger I will burn
if I step over the line
where the night and day divide.
So I remain in the twilight
shadowed and shrouded
in secrets.

~~~~~~~

Precious one

Your Soul is beautiful.
You have an inner light so radiant,
that it shines through,
in all your thoughts, deeds and actions.

You are never dimmed for long
even when others try and extinguish your light,
you only shine the brighter
When you refuse to become less than you are.

By Being,
alone,
you make the world a better place.

~~~~~~~

You will find me
in the thistledown
Floating gently by
To ephemeral to hold
But strong enough to fly

~~~~~~~

On the site of the sacred stone
there is a portal.
We will meet there at the appointed time.
My arms will be open to reach for you ,
my heart full as my eyes see you again.
Until then, I know you await me
in the shadows.
I cannot touch you
but know you are there all the same.
If I wait long enough,
You will come.

~~~~~~~

Carpe Noctem

Do not fear the silence of the night.
If you listen carefully,
you will hear the music of your soul,
in the liminal hours before the dawn.

~~~~~~~

Tribe is all
Our strands of Wyrd
making beautiful patterns
invisible to eye
seen by soul

~~~~~~~

I Think, Therefore I'm Spam
(an ode to social media)

All life is here
In spiteful microcosm

Send a kiss to those who will never receive it
Send words of hope they'll never believe it

Embittered psychopaths are free range
Relationships are virtually defunct
Cyber space has no empathy
The blessings you send are just the ghosts of
binary

The de-friended haunt you
While sociopaths taunt you

All life is here

~~~~~~~~

Carol for the Lonely

For every Christmas jingle
in the supermarket queue,
jarring, maddening and loud,
stuffed with false cheer,
at the loneliest time of the year.
They are a mockery now
a reminder of the past,
when Christmas was grand,
when family was all
and there were still people
seated around the table.
Turkey comes in a microwave meal,
for one.
No point of crackers
there is no one to pull them with.
Adverts come thick on the ground
from September now,
they burn my eyes
with unshed tears
for memories of better years.
The Salvation Army Band
play their hymns.
Children queue for Santa
with grandiose expectations,
a game machine
a laptop or an iPhone.
If I could be a child again,

I would sit on his lap
and tell him
my one wish.
That never want to be alone
for Christmas
when I am old.

~~~~~~~

I built my house
deep within the oak groves
at the centre of the forest.
With four towers marking
The cardinal points.

None may enter
unless by my displeasure.
Measures have been taken,
Sigel's have been cast,
to ward my home.

It is never lonely,
for my library is vast,
it contains many friends
old and new.
It is all I need.

~~~~~~~

How Soon the Seasons of the Soul Pass

When I met you, it was balmy like a summer
day,
as free as running through the gentle lapping
tide,
as uninhibited as the laughter of children,
rolling down dunes and digging in sand.

The rains came quickly after that, dampening
my ardour.
How soon it ended, this idyll of our season
when I saw the leaves fall from your hair,
at the same time the scales fell from my eyes.

Had I looked at the sky rather than into your
face
at the very beginning of us
I would have perhaps seen the storm clouds
gathering forebodingly on the horizon.

I should have taken shelter from your sun,
covered my heart in factor 50
so you couldn't penetrate it
and damage the skin of my soul.

~~~~~~~~

If you probe the undergrowth,
you will find me 'neath the moss.
Wasted like my opportunities

It is said, we all have a book in us.
You can read mine, on the lines of my face,
disgrace and neglect feature.

Pull back the bind weed
that strangled my ambition,
avoid the poison ivy of my dreams.
See yourself in the mirror of my eyes.

~~~~~~~

The time of the dead approaches.
The cycles which bind us to the land,
penetrate the mists
and pierce the veil between the worlds.
All is still at Samhain,
until you feel the frisson as the veil ripples.
The hand of your Ancestor upon your shoulder,
the whispers as they call you home.
The veil grows ever thinner
as you grow older.
Your cycle is ready to begin again.
On the day you are ready,
reach out and take the proffered hand
and go into the love of generations.

~~~~~~~~

'Step inside our ring of stones'
spoke whispers in the air
'Sit a while and rest your bones
within our realm so fair

To Tylwyth Teg our portal goes
It lies beneath the tree
just take our hand and come with us
unto the Western Sea

Eat our honeyed fairy bread
and drink deep of our ale
lay down on moss, your weary head
and listen to our tale

To Tylwyth Teg our portal goes
It lies beneath the tree
just take our hand and come with us
unto the Western Sea

You will not age, as humans do
and never know the pain
or feel the loss of passing love
when it begins to wane

To Tylwyth Teg our portal goes
It lies beneath the tree
just take our hand and come with us
unto the Western Sea'

~~~~~~~

Ode to Man From a Cave

Safe from birth,
within my womb,
until at last
I was their tomb.
I saw their pain and final hours,
heard weeping and smelled funeral flowers.
I watched them grow and laugh and sing,
as they conquered everything.
When their conscious grew much higher
Warmed them when they discovered fire.
At last I was abandoned when
they learned to build the homes of men.
But I await until they fall
when greed and war destroy them all,
They will come into my walls once more
and live within me as before.

~~~~~~~

Allfathers Lament

Come sit down and rest by the cool Well of Urd
Come traveller, and hear as you wait
We'll regale you with tales of the stories of old
Where the sisters of Wyrd weave your fate

Brave Odin he hanged from a branch of the tree
For nine nights he gazed at the moon
Great wisdom he found, while above the ground
And was given the lore of the runes

Come sit down and rest by the cool Well of Urd
Come traveller, and hear as you wait
We'll regale you with tales of the stories of old
Where the sisters of Wyrd weave your fate

He travelled the land to the Well of Mimir
For all knowledge from under the sky
He drank of the well, and fell under the spell
And the price asked of him was his eye

Come sit down and rest by the cool Well of Urd
Come traveller, and hear as you wait
We'll regale you with tales of the stories of old
Where the sisters of Wyrd weave your fate

Two ravens they came to land on the leaves
And spoke in his ear of all things

Memory and thought, the black creatures
brought
When he gave them the power to sing

Come sit down and rest by the cool Well of Urd
Come traveller, and hear as you wait
We'll regale you with tales of the stories of old
Where the sisters of Wyrd weave your fate

~~~~~~~

Fairy tunnels in the trees
Clouties dance upon the breeze
Wells are dressed in ribbons bright
Mummers come on May Day night

Bardic Chairs are lost and won
Draw down the moon and greet the sun
Wicker Men are set on fire
Beltane flames to fuel desire

Wassail cider, All Souls Eve
Dumb Suppers eaten while we grieve
Past, present, future, hand in hand
These are the customs of our land

~~~~~~~~

I see the faces in the trees,
I hear the whispers of the breeze.
Walk amongst the falling leaves
hear the tale the tall tree weaves.
Faerie tunnels, rings and bowers,
full of bushes, plants and flowers.
In periphery the Fae all dance,
drumming folk to tribal trance.

~~~~~~~

From yards of bone
to fields of stone,
the ancient pathways lead,
from cairn to cross
on ivy, moss,
the Spirits come to feed.
The leys are found beneath the sand,
in waterways that cross the land.
The Genius Loci whispers low,
his ghostly wisdom to bestow.

~~~~~~~

The trees watch through time
they do not judge,
merely whisper to each other.
They are givers to man,
of fruit and flower,
shade and shelter.
They are cut and maimed,
burned and broken,
yet still they endure.
Their leafy cloaks
doomed to fall and die,
to nourish the forest floor.

~~~~~~~

When empires rise and fall again
and only sacred sites remain.
Books and records, deeds of trust,
Have dried and fallen into dust.
Like some Universal plan,
again will come the rise of man.
We'll till the soil and plant the grain
and use the sacred sites again.

~~~~~~~~

Cauled in mystery,
seeped in history,
I stand alone
to guard the bone,
of those who lie beneath.
They go from Earth
to Odin's Hall,
the mightiest warrior
still must fall,
and blood doth cleanse the land.

~~~~~~~

It's mostly ephemera
with a touch of fluff,
mixed in with fairy dust
for effect,
and a large spoon to stir
the cauldron.

~~~~~~~

Darkness I Am

I roll down the shadowed stairs
before I catch you unawares,
I hide the moonbeams, trap the light
and keep you in eternal night.
I am the twilight, early come,
I worship stars and block out sun.
The firefly and the glow-worm's friend,
A dark eclipse without an end.

~~~~~~~

I love this land my forefathers walked
From the heather and the broom
To the Neolithic tomb
The wooded pools and waterfalls
These rolling hills, the windswept coasts
The hamlets of ancestral ghosts

~~~~~~~

Join me at the table dear
We'll sit and eat in silence
Make sure to eat your mushroom soup
Or I'll resort to violence

~~~~~~~

We are lost, broken children,
huddled together for warmth.
Our souls connected
by strings which stretch,
but never quite break.

As a tribe we are strong.
Alone we are less than nothing,
yearning for a place to belong.
Knowing we may never
meet in this lifetime.

But still we hope and dream.

~~~~~~~~

Embittered Yule

Thousands of stars sparkle on trees
and the eaves of houses.
They mask the sadness behind
the closed doors.
The fighting put aside
for the festive period
festering on low boil
next to the sprouts.
Marriages as stale as the turkey
in the New Years Eve curry,
are revived briefly
for the sake of the relatives.
Lonely Aunts and Uncles
who are relegated back to
the nursing homes and council bungalows
On Boxing Day,
are on day release once a year,
They sit in the arm chair,
like spectres at the feast.
Feeling as unwanted
as the satsumas and nuts
in the Christmas stockings,
hung on the mantelpiece
along with the lost hopes and dreams
of those doomed to repeat their mistakes
year in year out.
Usher in the fake bonhomie

with the box of tinsel from the attic.
When old acquaintances should be forgot
for the sake of our self-respect.
When you're a pay-day away from bankruptcy
just to fund a lie
and the children tire of the toy
before the batteries have run down
and the arguing starts again.

~~~~~~~

I hold you in my heart,
it feels like drawing breath
for the first time.
Naked and stripped to my soul,
so close that
I don't know where I end
and you begin.

Engulfed by the shadows
I used to fear,
they comfort me now
and the very walls that surrounded me
became a womb,
a sanctuary,
where once they were
my prison.

My arms enfold you
and the void within
is filled momentarily
until you tear yourself away,
and I am empty again.
A lonely child,
bereft of love.
Broken.

~~~~~~~

How easily your gentle soul is maimed.
Your hope flutters in my palm,
until I crush it slowly
in my fist
along with your dreams.
If you asked me "Why?"
I would say
that you are at fault
for loving me.

~~~~~~~

Ophelia Trilogy

~~

Dream of Ophelia

You say I will find you beneath the flowers.
I will be bound in rushes
and anointed with water lilies,
A willing sacrifice to the naiad.
The water will carry me to the sea,
for my body cannot bear
the shame of the iron
that you would stake me with.
My soul will ride the waves,
the reflection of the moon
will pull me in its tide,
into silver forgetfulness.
The cloudy notion that remains
of our time together in the sun
will soon pass,
when I drink from the Lethe
It will quell the pain,
as I will cease to remember
even that.
When the blossom
which once graced your crown
floats upon becalmed waters,
I will not see your face

again.

~~~~~~~

Ophelia Shadowed

I am drowning
tendrils of weed
wrapping my wrists,
pulling me deeper
like my dreams.

Semi-conscious,
I walk towards
the rivers edge,
beguiled
by the spirit of the place.

The water feels warm
and comforting,
like coming home.
The Naiad embraces me
death is my friend.

~~~~~~~

Ophelia's Dirge

The reality is not the same.
I will not be beautiful beneath the water.
The rushes will not bear me on a bier upstream
lit by sunbeams
with a waterlily wreath.
No comforting arms to wait for me in the
beyond
just the undertow to tug me down
in an inky black void.
No poet will know of my passing,
my tale will be untold.
The jewelled fish of the deep will not be my
companions
Instead, they will feast on my remains.
Nobody to mourn me, not a tear at my grave
there will be no lover weeping
at the prow of a darkly draped boat.
Not a single red rose will be cast
on the waters of my grave.

~~~~~~~~

Luna of the silver mists

Maybe you were born under an auspicious star?
You are woven from moonbeams
and they wreath you in a quiet, pale light.
The benighted flock to you like moths to a
flame
and become butterflies in your ethereal glow.
Your soul is older than time,
it belongs to the seasons and the tides.
You are cloaked in history's mists,
your origins as mysterious as
half-forgotten fables,
To me, you are more real than life itself.

~~~~~~~~

The night is my eiderdown,
I draw it around me
like a cloak, to comfort me.

It is made of dreams and wishes.
I embroider it with stars
and wash it in moonlight.

It will not fade
like my expectations.

~~~~~~~

Morrigan I Am

Lady of the darkness,
comforter of the dead.
On all the battlefields of all wars.
I can only love you at the end.
But will cover you with my embrace,
to end your suffering.
Oh I weep for you then,
like a star-crossed lover.
Doomed only to meet you
for a moment in time.
It is my curse
and my blessing,
the two are entwined.
Your soul flies' home
on my cry of grief.

~~~~~~~

Lady of the Hollow Ways

Deep among the tangle of the trees
I come to find you,
where the river runs over the flat stones
eternally
And waterfalls sparkle
in the flickers of the sun,
through dappled shade.
Hollow ways are your home,
mysterious and beautiful
like your soul.

You were too kind
for this cruel world,
so you took to the crossroads
and the hedges,
haunting the
places where the dark and light
divide.
I see you in flashes
when I touch the ancient stones.
You are clothed in the the green of the trees,
crowned by the thorns of sadness,
insubstantial as a shade.

I saw your reflection
looking back at me
in the crystal waters of a pool.

You were close then,
a peripheral thing,
veiled from my eyes.
The ripples of the water
blurred your face
as I touched you
with my hand.
Then you vanished,
leaving me alone with my pain.
My quest for you
is my comfort.

~~~~~~~

Broken like china
although I was never that fine.
I cannot be put back together
although I have tried
and will never cease
attempting to put
the painful shards
in their place.
They cut me
when I pick them up
and my tears mingle
with the blood they draw,
yet I still I try to repair myself.

Some pieces
were crushed to powder
underfoot,
deliberately
with calculation.
I am not so innocent
in my treatment of myself.
I have handed my heart to you
to break all over again,
many times.
A lesson never learned
despite the failures.

~~~~~~~~

For once,
I would like to be beautiful,
just for a second,
to taste what it is like
to be adored.
Rather than eating crumbs
from the table.

Even that is utility,
not inlaid with marquetry.
Laminated with pain,
scarred with use
that no amount of polish
can hide.

~~~~~~~

Rejection

I feel it all the days of my life
insidious and mocking.
Lurking to strike again,
like a serial killer
in a foggy alleyway.

It is an unwanted companion
yet I cannot shake it off.
Although it is unsubstantial
in the eyes of others.
to me it is a nightmare
of epic proportions.

I look for it always
inviting it at times,
rather than it taking me unaware.
But it is always there.

~~~~~~~

We were as captive
as the rhino in the room with us
and just as endangered
by the flame we ignited in each other.
The heat, so intense, that it burned all around
us
to scorched earth.
Even time and distance couldn't extinguish it
although we tried, so hard, to pour cold water
on it.
Maybe we should get our fingers burned?
Give in and walk into the flames?
Resisting it hurts more than the pain of the
inferno.

~~~~~~~

You cannot love too much
but you can love unconditionally.
Do not expect a return
it was never quid pro quo,
just be thankful if it happens.
Be mindful always.
Finer feelings can be well hidden
and damaged easily.
We are all fragile
under the armour we wear.

~~~~~~~

Hope is a four-letter word

Let me go
to that beautiful place
that exists in my mind,
where it is safe
and free of hatred.
I can visit when reality
becomes too much.

Yet I am drawn back to life
to face the mundane.
Where colour is muted
and tinged with sadness.
Where people are
devoid of empathy
and cruel.

At times my oasis
is hard to find.
I can navigate by the stars
and find it in my dreamscape.
But sometimes the toxic rays
of everyday living,
taint it with sadness.

~~~~~~~~

I sculpt myself
using clay over bones.
Every stroke hurts so much
that some days, it takes courage to try.

Sometimes I add glitter
and other days I add tears,
both sparkle
in the light of the sun.

Passion is never lacking
in my craft.
Motivation comes and goes,
along with confidence.

There are times I create something
misshapen and twisted,
but I can cut that way
and begin again.

And create the person
I want to be.

~~~~~~~~

Think outside the box,
as there are no corners
to back yourself into.
Colour outside the lines,
always.

Be unique.
Be special.

Do not conform
to society's narrow perceptions.
You will not be loved more
if you pretend,
to be something you are not.

Dance in the light of the moon
and in the rays of the sun.
Use the music in your soul
to dance to your own tune.

~~~~~~~

My blanket fort
is warm and safe,
Come in!
Sit down, and I will spin
tales of old
to entertain you.

Let your weary bones
sink into the silk cushions.
Forget your age,
It is but a number
anyhow.

Be a child again
as we journey
through enchanted forests
and faerie glens.

When your eyelids grow heavy,
open your mind's eye
and see the colours of the rainbow
dancing through the clouds.
The unicorn will come if you call
tame to your hand,
as you are pure of heart.

~~~~~~~~

Hidden in-between worlds,
never belonging to either.
I forged my own Awen,
in the heat of my failure
and misery.

I fed the fire of creation
with my rejection.
Piece by piece
until it burned
brightly.

Words came easily then,
wounding and scarring
They tattooed my soul
then flowed onto the page
from my pen.

Longing and yearning
were hidden between the lines,
betwixt regret and bitterness.
You can find them
if you look closely enough.

But you never cared to.

~~~~~~~

I wear rejection like a shroud
pulled around me in misery,
yet, like the King's new clothes,
it is invisible to the naked eye.
Unless you saw inside my soul
you would miss it.

It is in my eyes too,
you just never
looked deeply enough
to see it.
It is there every time
you break a promise
and I die a little bit more.

~~~~~~~~

I wander in the labyrinth
of my imagination.
Drifting through daydreams
and wading through nightmares,
that ensnare me with threads
from spider's webs.
There is no escape
from my dreamscape.

~~~~~~~

Sometimes I feel
like I have spent my life
swimming against the tide

Trying to fit in
when I should be apart
and alone

It is better thus
none can strike at my heart
and wound me

Save myself

~~~~~~~

What is freedom?
A concept maybe?
Something I will never obtain
as I cannot escape
from myself
only into imagination
where spectres await.
They live in my soul
and sit at my every feast
lurking,
as I try my wings
and find them broken.
Chains shackle me
to reality,
I forged them
just as surely
as did Marley's Ghost.
They weigh heavily on my mind
binding me to
a lonely existence.

I fear and love life
in equal measure.
Repelled by normality
and intoxicated by dreams.
No bravery in my heart
exists
to allow me to escape
or die trying.

I cannot conform
nor do I want to.
For pain brings
its own reward,
It gives birth to
the wellspring of words
within.

~~~~~~~

Myth and Magic
surround me
in perpetual mist.
Memorising and enticing
ephemeral,
but more real to me
than the common life.
It entices me in
and grips my being,
while I watch the Norns
my fate in their hands.
Oft times they mock
but I am still ensnared
by their enchantment,
while they spin, weave and cut
as they wish.
Who I was
Who I am
And who I shall be
is in their hands
as much as it is in mine.
I only choose
how I shall walk that path
to the destination they decide.

~~~~~~~

When all seems to be falling apart,
look to the single weed
pushing through the concrete
to be a symbol of hope
of our survival,
in a hostile environment.
It is as tenacious in its will
as we must be.

~~~~~~~

Can you hear the dragonflies?
They are skipping on the surface
of the water
in the sunbeams.
You need to stop and listen
shut out the distractions
of everyday life
and become part of nature
again.

Can you count the colours?
Gold on green, shot through with purple
gleaming like jewels.
The amethyst and emerald
vying to catch your eye,
like the rainbow
which brings hope after the storm.

Can you smell the flowers?
More beautiful than bottles of scent,
fragile and bending in the wind
but strong enough to endure.
Jasmine and freesias
mix with the roses and honeysuckle
to delight your senses.
All you need to do, is pause
and drink in your surroundings.

~~~~~~~

If I asked you
"What do you want from me?"
I suspect the truthful answer
would be "Nothing".
But you ghost me instead
leaving me hopeful.
Cruelty seems to come naturally
to you

~~~~~~~

In dreams
you are all I could want you to be
and more.
You pulled the sword
from the stone of my heart
and dubbed yourself
my protector
against all who wish me harm.
You are warm and loving there,
your arms, my shelter
against the storms.
We are closer than
twins in the womb
in that twilight world.
If it were possible
to take a draught
of living death,
so I could remain there
with you always,
I would do so willingly.

~~~~~~~

It is not mine
to forgive you.
You did nought
but create me
and name me,
then abandon me
to a fate worse
than that which
you would have
handed to me,
had you kept me.

~~~~~~~

Printed in Great Britain
by Amazon

82570224R00099